THE LITTLE MERMAID

Princess Stories Starring Ariel

Adapted by Wendy Wax and Rita Balducci

Illustrated by Disney Storybook Artists

CONTENTS

Reader's Digest
Children's Books

Pleasantville, New York • Montréal, Québec • Bath, United Kingdom

The Little Mermaid

Deep under the sea, a royal concert was about to begin. King Triton had invited all the merpeople to hear his youngest daughter, Ariel, sing with her sisters. Sebastian the crab had great confidence in Ariel's debut, and his chest swelled with pride as a clamshell popped open to reveal...nothing. Ariel had forgotten about the concert!

DISK I

Instead, she was busy exploring the wreck of a sunken ship with her fish friend Flounder. They suddenly got a big surprise.

"Shark!" Flounder shouted in a panic. Ariel and Flounder escaped just in time.

But they weren't entirely out of

3 danger. The evil sea witch Ursula had been watching them from a magic bubble. Ursula hated King Triton and began to plot against him. "King Triton's daughter may be very useful to me," Ursula decided.

King Triton was furious about Ariel missing the concert. When he found out she had been up to the surface of the sea, he knew something had to be done. The king believed that the surface was a dangerous place. He put Sebastian in charge of keeping Ariel out of trouble.

Ariel swam to her hidden cave. "I wish

4 I could know what it would be like to live on land," she sighed. She had treasures that she had collected from sunken ships, but they only gave her a glimpse of what humans were really like.

Ariel looked up to see the shadow of a ship overhead. "Ariel, wait!" cried Sebastian, but it was too late.

Ariel watched as sailors sang and danced on the ship's deck. She couldn't help noticing a handsome young man among them.

"Happy birthday, Prince Eric," said an older man as he unveiled a statue of the dashing prince.

5

Suddenly, a storm blew in. Lightning flashed and the wind howled. Ariel watched as the ship tossed in the waves. Prince Eric was thrown overboard!

Ariel dove under the water and pulled the unconscious prince to shore. She had never been so close to a human before. She

6 sang to him softly until he began to wake up. Just then, a dog's barking startled her, and she quickly slipped back into the sea.

"There was a girl," the prince told his friend, Sir Grimsby. "She had the most beautiful voice. She saved me." He had fallen in love with the mysterious young woman.

Ariel had fallen in love, too. King Triton noticed how

happy she was, but when he learned that she had disobeyed him and saved a human, he lost his temper. With one

7

wave of his arm, King Triton destroyed all of Ariel's treasures.

Ariel was quite upset with her father. *He doesn't understand me or that I must follow my own heart. And my heart leads me to Prince Eric. I must see the prince again,* Ariel thought, *even if I have to go to Ursula to do it!*

Ursula told Ariel that

she could become a human for three days. At the end of that time, the prince would have to give her a kiss of true love if she were to remain with him always.

"And if he doesn't, you turn back into a mermaid, and you belong to me!" Ursula cackled. "Oh, yes, we must talk about the

8

price. You must give me...your voice!"

Ariel knew that Ursula could not be trusted, but she longed to be with Prince Eric once more. She signed the agreement. Immediately, she began to change. Her tail

turned into legs, and she could no longer breathe underwater. She swam to the surface, gasping for air. When Ariel reached the shallow waters offshore, she

DISK 2

9

gazed in wonder at her new legs.

Ariel discovered that life on land was even more exciting than she had ever dreamed. *So this is what it is like to have legs!* Ariel thought.

Prince Eric was instantly enchanted with Ariel. He invited her to stay at the palace and took her for a

10 tour of the kingdom. Ariel desperately wished there was some way to let him know who she really was. Time was running out!

Flounder, Sebastian, and Scuttle the seagull tried to help the romance along. Sebastian crooned a love song as Prince

11 Eric leaned over to kiss Ariel. Suddenly, their boat tipped over! Flotsam and Jetsam, Ursula's pet eels, had ruined the lovely moment.

"That was too close," Ursula decided. She came ashore disguised as a beautiful woman to distract Eric. Using Ariel's voice  and her own hypnotic power, she tricked the prince into thinking that she was the one who had rescued him.

"We will be married today," Eric said, falling under her spell. He took the hand of his bride-to-be. Ariel was heartbroken. She sat on the dock and watched as the wedding ship sailed off into the sunset.

Scuttle flew over the ship and recognized Ursula on board. When Ariel learned the true identity of the woman Eric planned to marry, she knew she had to stop the wedding.

As the ceremony began, flocks of seagulls attacked the wedding party. The shell which held Ariel's voice was torn from Ursula's necklace. Ariel's voice escaped and returned to Ariel.

"Eric!" Ariel cried. Ursula's spell was broken. The prince realized that Ariel was the woman who had saved him. He leaned forward to kiss her.

"You're too late!" shrieked Ursula as huge, black tentacles burst forth from her body. Ursula grabbed Ariel, who had turned back into a mermaid, and pulled her under the water.

King Triton tried to stop Ursula from taking his daughter. "Take me instead," he said. Ursula agreed. With the king's trident in hand, she became huge.

14

15

Then suddenly Prince Eric steered the bow of the ship right into Ursula, putting an end to her forever.

When King Triton saw how deeply Ariel and Eric loved each other, he knew he had no choice but to grant them their wish to be married. He changed Ariel back into a human, and with humans and merpeople looking on, Ariel and Eric were married at sea. At last, Ariel's dreams had come true!

16

THE LITTLE MERMAID

Ariel in: The Music of Love

I have a surprise for you!" Flounder said to his best friend, Princess Ariel. He grabbed her hands and started to swim in circles.

"I love surprises! What is it? Give me a hint, Flounder," said Ariel.

"You won't believe it. It's so amazing, I need a band of buglers just to announce it! Follow me."

But Sebastian objected. After all, they were in the middle of a rehearsal for his latest musical extravaganza, and Ariel was the lead singer. "Where are you going?" he called after them.

"It's just a five-minute break," reasoned Ariel. "Flounder has something he needs to show me." She flashed him a smile.

"Unbelievable!" muttered Sebastian. "Young people these days don't know about work...."

♫ Play Song 3 Flounder led Ariel over to a statue of a handsome human he had found on a shipwreck. "Ta da!" he said.

"Prince Eric!" Ariel exclaimed. "I love it!"

"You mean you love him," said Flounder.

"Shhh," said Ariel. "You're the only one who

knows. If my father finds out, he'll be furious."

She swam around the statue, taking in every detail. She imagined gazing into the dreamy eyes of Prince Eric. She had only seen him once on a sinking ship. He probably had no idea that she had been the one to save him from drowning.

"Ariel, shouldn't you be getting back to rehearsal?" Flounder asked. But Ariel's mind was elsewhere. She imagined marrying Prince Eric. In order to walk down the aisle, she'd have to get herself a pair of legs and feet. They'd have a romantic wedding at the water's edge so her family could be there to watch. Her father, King Triton, would be there, smiling proudly—after all, this was only a daydream. Her older sisters would be there, too. She wondered how the prince's family would feel about having merfolk as relatives. Some humans, she'd been told, didn't believe they existed. But if Prince Eric loved her, so would his family.

"Ariel!" Sebastian called from several feet away. "Come back!"

Play Song 4 But Ariel was planning the menu and didn't hear anyone else. First, they would serve trays of whipped seaweed on crackers and blue sea-grass wraps. She hurried through the soups, salads, and main courses, so she could get to the best part—the wedding cake. It would be huge and pretty, with tiny statues of herself and Prince Eric.

"Yoo hoo! Ari-ellll!" called Sebastian. "We must rehearse!"

Play Song 5 He didn't get an answer because Ariel was busy deciding what to wear to her wedding. After much thought, she decided on a shimmering veil, a tiara, and yellow sea stars in her hair. She imagined Flounder bringing her strands of pearls that he borrowed from the most distinguished family of oysters.

"There you are!" Sebastian said, swimming toward Ariel. "I'm not going to let you get away this time."

"Sebastian!" Ariel said, finally hearing him. "If we don't swim fast, we're going to be late for my wedding."

"Huh?" said Sebastian, feeling very confused. "Wedding? What wedding?"

Play Song 6
"What's going on?" a member of the orchestra asked.

"Ariel thinks she's having some sort of wedding," grumbled Sebastian. "I guess we could hold the rehearsal here." But before he could give them the signal, Ariel cleared her throat. She had an announcement to make.

"I, Ariel, take Prince Eric to be my lawful, wedded husband," she said happily. "I love him with all my heart."

Flounder couldn't help gazing at Ariel with admiration.

Play
Song
7
"You make a beautiful bride," he said. "Prince Eric is the luckiest human in the world."

Even Sebastian felt teary-eyed as he led the orchestra in a fantasy-wedding musical number.

"Now will you sing, Ariel?" an exhausted Sebastian pleaded with her. "Please?!"

"I have one last thing to do," said Ariel. With that, she flung a bouquet of seaweed. Flounder swam to catch it.